P9-CDZ-854

At 8:50 a.m. on September 11, 2001, I looked up from my drawing table and saw in the distance an enormous plume of smoke rising high above and beyond the Empire State Building. I soon learned that the smoke covering the city came from the twin towers of the World Trade Center.

After a few days, I went to Union Square—to be closer to the communal outpouring of anguish in the city. I saw the roses, and learned how they came to be there. Relying on memory and imagination, I wrote and illustrated <u>September Roses</u> the following spring.

September Roses

Jeanette Winter

Frances Foster Books
Farrar Straus Giroux · New York

As I looked down at the roses,
a young man walked to where I stood
and told me how they came to be there.

Far away in South Africa, he said,
across the ocean,

over mountains,

beyond the desert,

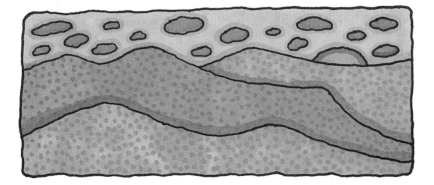

two sisters lived together
and grew roses.

Their greenhouse overflowed with roses of every kind~ red roses, pink roses, yellow roses.

Roses surrounded their little house

and brightened every room.

Every night the sisters
worked on designs
for their rose display

at the flower show,
far away
in New York City.

When the designs were finished,
they carefully packed 2,400 roses.

It was time for the journey.

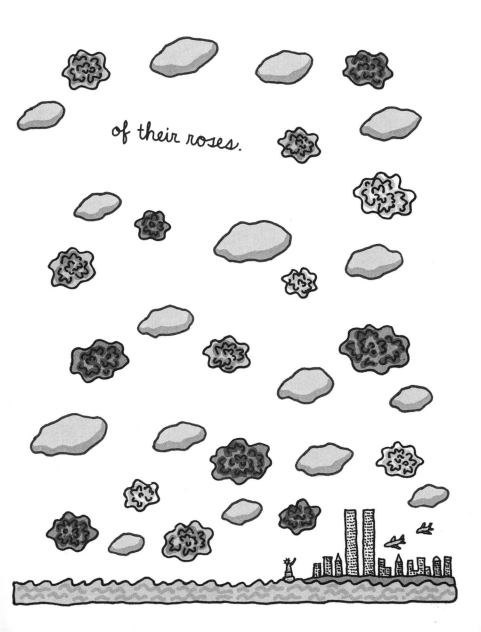

of their roses.

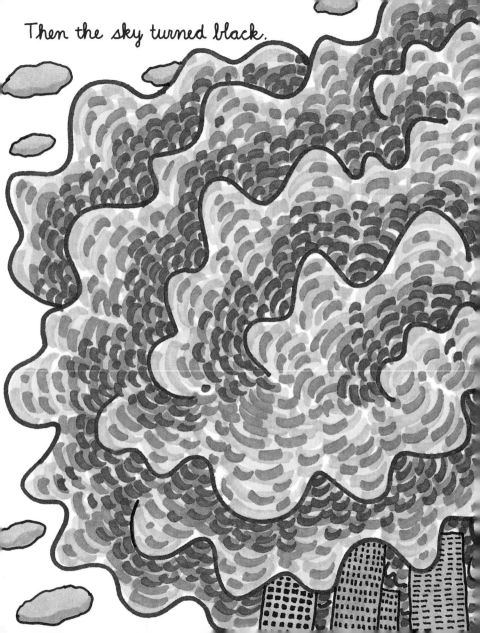

Then the sky turned black.

Their airplane landed.

There were tears enough

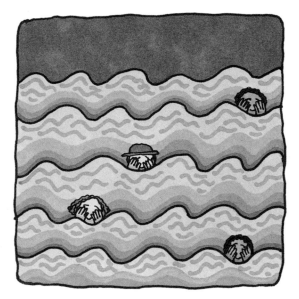

to fill an ocean.

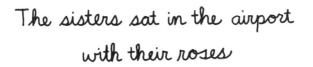

The sisters sat in the airport
with their roses

PERISHABLE

TOWERS FALL ... FIRE

PERISHABLE

all day

and all night.

There was no place for them to go.

The sisters knew what to do.
They found an empty space
on the grass

and set to work—

placing one rose next to another,
and another, their hands
moving quickly.

The grass was soon covered
with roses.

when the sisters stepped back,

there lay the fallen towers.

My tears

fell on the roses.

The story recorded here is as I had originally envisioned it.

I subsequently learned the following specifics: The two women, commercial rose growers in South Africa, came to New York to attend the Agriflowers & Floritech Expo USA. The flower show was called off, the hotels were full, and all flights home were canceled. Stranded at LaGuardia Airport with over two thousand roses, the two women were given lodging by members of the First United Methodist Church of Flushing, New York, who had come to the airport to offer shelter to those in need.

www.fsgkidsbooks.com

Winter, Jeanette.
    September roses / Jeanette Winter.— 1st ed.
        p. cm.
    Summary: On September 11, 2001, two sisters from South Africa find good use for the roses they have grown when the flower show in New York City is canceled due to the attack on the World Trade Center.
    ISBN 0-374-36736-1
    [1. September 11 Terrorist Attacks, 2001—Fiction. 2. World Trade Center (New York, N.Y.)—Fiction. 3. Roses—Fiction. 4. Gardens—Fiction. 5. Sisters—Fiction. 6. New York (N.Y.)—Fiction.] I. Title.

PZ7.W7547Se 2004
[E]—dc22
                                                                            2003054877